GAY FOR PAY

SAM JD HUNT

Gay for Pay
Copyright © 2017 by Sam JD Hunt

Published in the United States of America

First Published, 2017
Cover design by Sam JD Hunt
Cover images © Depositphoto

Intended for mature 18+ readers only.

Caleb Drake is going down.
Which is why he's *going down*.

Caleb Drake is a guy's guy—beer on Friday, football on Sunday, he couldn't be more secure in his sexuality. But he *is* dealing with the aftermath of an expensive divorce, and his shaky judgment has caused him to lose his lucrative career as a personal injury attorney. Facing disbarment, and costly legal fees, he considers an unthinkable solution offered by an unlikely advisor: his ex-wife.

John Butters is in town, trolling Las Vegas for gay-for-pay performers for his hit direct-to-internet porn series, *Butter Me Up*. In the back of his van or in a hotel room, Butters films everyday straight guys who are willing to go *there* for cash.

Butter's newest find, the ridiculously endowed Caleb, is a sure hit. With more and more cash on the line, Caleb goes further and further until a blast from his past turns his universe upside down—his former college roommate Derek Johnson.

A bisexual romp of an erotic romantic comedy, *Gay for Pay* will leave you asking, "What the hell did I just read?"

A story so wrong it has to be right from the author of *Taken by Two*.

"The Edge... there is no honest way to explain it because the only people who really know where it is are the ones who have gone over."
Hunter S. Thompson

"I only invite intellects, wordsmiths, crazy bitches, broken people, and lust-monsters to my tea party."
Erin Van Vuren

Dedicated to the reader who craves something different.

I admit it felt good when his lips wrapped around my cock. *Really* good. When I started the scene, I told myself I'd pretend it was a chick blowing me. But as his tongue stroked the underside of the head, I struggled to think about any chick, or anyone but him sucking me off. He was so fucking *skilled* at it. This guy, Chad I think his name was, loved my dick down his throat—he wasn't rushing, he wasn't gagging —he was savoring it. That dude rolled his tongue up and down my ten-inch cock like it was a fucking lollipop.

By the time he swallowed, taking the whole thing down his tight throat like no girl had ever done, I was about to shoot my wad. *Think about war, sick babies, puppies, think about anything...* But when the director barked at the guy to play with my balls, I was done. That afternoon in some hotel room in Vegas with cameras rolling, I had the best blowjob of my life. I was hooked.

But let me back up a little and tell you how I got there. Everything about that blistering summer is seared into my memory, and for some reason, I'm writing it all down.

ONE
LONG DUCK DONG

"YOU HAVE to share that giant cock with the world."

"I'm trying to, baby, one pussy at a time." My wife, I mean my ex-wife, Jill, stared at me as I stroked off in front of her. It was our favorite pastime since she stopped letting me fuck her a month ago.

"Shit, Cal," she moaned as her manicured fingers dipped into the waistband of her skirt. As had become our sick little routine, her eyes locked onto my throbbing cock as I pumped it harder and faster until a glistening layer of my own spunk spread out across my belly.

"Next time, either you let me touch you or it's not happening, Jill," I snapped after she'd fingered herself off, all under the shroud of her fucking pencil skirt.

I kid you not, it wasn't more than two minutes later, her fingers still wet and barely out of her warm snatch, when she started nagging me again about shit. "Give me my money, Caleb," she said, her tone colder than Lake Superior in January.

"Seriously, Jill? You are about to marry Joe Fucking Money Bags and you're still shaking me down for money? AFTER watching me jerk off?"

"Cal, don't make me take you to court. You know I'll win."

"You won't—I'm a better lawyer, baby doll."

"Better? Did you forget you are about to be disbarred?"

I took a deep breath—I was about to break and didn't need her to see it. "I'll write you a check."

She shook her head. "Cash, your last check bounced all the way to Reno."

Jill left with the stack of money I needed to give the repo guy that afternoon. Yeah, that's right, not only was I behind on whatever I owed Jill, but I was also way behind on my car payments. To make my day even shittier, the second Jill's 'Vette left my driveway my maid Kennedy popped down the stairs. Yes, Kennedy—they name young women after presidents nowadays it seems.

"That was disgusting," she said with a sneer.

"Why the fuck were you eavesdropping? You're supposed to be cleaning my damn house."

"I thought we were hanging out. Last night was hot, right?"

"Hanging out? What does that mean?"

"You are so old," she said with a sigh, her feather duster dancing down my handrail.

"I'm not old—I'm thirty-five, sweetheart. And last night was fine, but we aren't like going steady or anything."

She shook her head at me. "O-L-D. And you owe me fifty bucks for today."

"Sorry, kid, I just gave all my cash to the horny ex."

She stared at me for a minute, her eyes drifting toward my still half-hard bulge. "You should start a YouTube channel," she finally said. "My friend does that and she makes a fortune from it."

"YouTube? And do what—give legal advice from Las Vegas' most prominent about-to-be disbarred attorney?"

"No, it has to be sex stuff silly," she said, wiggling past me with that fine, ready-to-be-fucked-again ass of hers.

"Your friend does that?"

"Yeah, she puts up vids of herself with dildos, vibrators, that sort of thing. You have an awesome dick, Cal—use it to dig yourself out of your cash crisis."

"Reagan, Kennedy, Nixon, whoever you are—I may be a disgrace, but I'm not ready to just chuck it all to get nasty on the internet."

"Very funny. Listen, you do it anonymously. Only show yourself from the waist down, or...well the neck down, it would be a shame not to show those killer abs. But literally, your fat nine-inch dick would get like thousands of clicks."

"Yeah, sure, whatever. Listen, I'll pay you double next time."

"Think about the YouTube thing. Oh hey, do you have anything to smoke? Maybe we can repeat last night?"

"Goodbye, kid," I said, escorting her from my way-too-massive-for-one-person suburban house. But, Jill's prophetic words still ran through my head: *You have to share that giant cock with the world.*

So I probably should slow down a little—I'm not good at this, I've never really written anything before for other people to read. Derek thinks it might make a good memoir, so whatever, I'll try. And we'll get to Derek later, much

later. For now I'll just tell you that my name is Caleb
Andrew Drake, and I know you want some backstory—how
did I become a divorced, drunk, disgraced mess of a man?
But you'll have to be patient with me; I just can't go there
now. My mind is a jumbled mess.

I *will* tell you about the night before I jacked off for Jill,
though. Even though Kennedy is an airheaded college
student, she is a most excellent fuck. Way better than the
uptight Jill Morgan who divorced me to marry some old rich
judge with a shriveled up gherkin for a dick.

So that night, Kennedy came over under the guise of
having left some earring at my house cleaning the week
prior, but it didn't take her long to seek me out on my
balcony and freely indulge in my best weed. Weed I
couldn't afford, I should add. And before you think that is
what got me in trouble, think again. Sin City allows recre-
ational marijuana use.

So anyway, she smokes with me, drinks with me, one
thing leads to another and before I know it, my lips are
wrapped around her massive tits right there on my balcony
with the sound of the pool sloshing all around. It was beautiful. Kennedy even did something Jill would never even
watch on porn—she took all ten inches up her tight ass. And
yes, she said *nine* but trust me, it's *ten*—I've been stroking
that monster my entire life, I should know. My hand barely
fits around it, but she took it all the way like a champ, with
cooking oil, no less. It's all I had—I'd used up all the
Astroglide the night before.

But that following afternoon, after the thing with Jill
and giving her all my cash, I wasn't in the mood for a tight
piece of ass. I was in the mood to dig myself out of the financial hole I was in. The repo guy didn't come for my car, so I

grabbed a tumbler of whiskey and headed out to my pool deck with my trusty MacBook.

Setting up a YouTube channel was easy, but pulling my dick out in public wasn't. Flaccid City every time I tried to make a video. What the actual fuck, I'd been jacking off in front of Jill forever, and I liked it. I loved being watched, I loved the wide, appreciative eyes running up and down the length of my dick. But now, with just me and the camera, not so much. So yeah, you know by now I'm an idiot. I texted Jill.

I knew just what would get her to leave Judge Wapner and hightail it back here.

I found the pendant, come get it before it gets stolen by the maid.

Sure enough, within minutes she was at my doorstep. Her stilettos clicked along the tile floor as she followed me into my house. What used to be *our* house. The suburban house she thought she wanted, to house the babies she told herself she was supposed to have—too bad it was all a big lie. And yeah, I was a total idiot for trying to keep the house. It's the main reason I'm up shit creek financially.

"Oh, yeah, it wasn't your grandmother's diamond, sorry, it was just some fake bauble the girl I fucked last week must have dropped," I lied.

I did get some satisfaction in the way her red-stained lips pulled to the side when I mentioned being with someone else. She still wanted me. Just not enough.

"Stop playing games, Cal."

"It's what I do best." I reached for her, only to have her pull back toward the wall. "Okay, listen, the truth is I need your help."

"You need a lot of help. I'm going home—Michael expects me at the gala thing tonight."

"Yeah, I was supposed to go but didn't feel like being stared at all night. But listen, it's not a big thing. I want you to watch me jack off again."

Her knees went together—she was turned on. "Uh, why?"

"I have this kink, don't judge. I want to video myself doing it." I knew she'd bite—I was the kinky one, and she loved it.

"So get a tripod," she said, but her knees were still locked together, and her eyes drifted to the bulge in my jeans.

"I tried alone, and I just can't do it. I need you, baby, I've always needed you."

She softened and reached for my iPhone. "I'm not even going to ask why, but whatever. I get to keep a copy, and it's a deal."

That afternoon, with Jill pointing my phone camera at me, something changed. When she was watching, I could perform. I teased the camera, played with it—I stroked off not for me, but for them. Putting on a show with my giant penis seemed to be something I actually did well, and by the time I was ready to explode so was Jill.

Although, unlike before, her fingers didn't reach for her needy pussy. This time, after she'd put my phone down, she came over and sat on my lap like she used to. "What the fuck happened to us, Jill?" I buried my face in her hair.

"It all just got to be too much with you, Cal. You're like a super nova, and I need stability, security. The thing with that girl was the last straw."

I pulled back from her. She still didn't believe me. "There was no *thing*. Bye, Jill."

She stood and looked down at me. My junk was still hanging out, leaking from the tip in the ultimate insult. "Come to the gala tonight, Cal. You're not out of the game yet—go and talk to the judge. Get him drunk—you're good at that."

Minutes after she left, I texted her the video and posted it to YouTube.

Jerking off with her holding the camera was easy; it was a rush, a thrill—and the second I posted it the likes started rolling in. And the comments... Holy shit, I went from feeling like a loser to the world's hottest guy in minutes. They wanted more.

One of the comments caught my attention. It was from a dude, and said:

I'll give you a hundred bucks to stroke off with your finger up your ass.

Well, that's fabulous LongDuckDong89, I thought, *but I'll pass.* But the offer of cash for the breaching of my virgin pooper did bring up an interesting question—how do I make money from these posts? I texted Kennedy, who ignored me.

As the comments rolled in, I did some Googling and learned how to set my new channel up for something called monetization. Of course I had to lie about my content, but within minutes I was ready to make a quick buck. It didn't have to last, it just had to earn me some quick cash to get Jill and the repo man off my back.

Just as I was about to stream some porn to get in the mood to make another video, my phone rang. It was Jill—actually calling me versus sending a text. I braced myself—she only called when she wanted something.

"That was *hot!*" she gushed from the other end of the line.

"You watched it happen, baby. What do you want?"

"It was different watching it on the video. Holy shit, Cal, I had to pull out the rabbit."

"Good to know. Listen, I'm a little busy..."

"I want you to come to the thing tonight. The judge said—"

"Do you not think it's fucking twisted that you call your almost husband *the judge?*"

"*Michael*, then, said he wanted to talk to you about your situation. Let him help, Cal. Get out of this mess for all of our sakes."

"You can both kiss my ass." I hung up. I didn't need help from the rickety old man who stole my wife.

TWO
THE VOMIT-EATING RODENT

I HAD zero intention of going to that fucking black-tie event, and would never stoop to getting help from her husband, The Honorable Michael Allen. When my best buddy got back to LA from his extended vacation in Cancun I'd ask him. Danny would help, I decided. He'd represent me in front of the Bar. But as for now, after I looked at my YouTube channel one more time, I decided to celebrate the nearly thousand likes my little jack-off scene had already generated.

Yeah, it was mid-afternoon, but hey, it was five o'clock somewhere. I went out to the booze fridge in the garage—everyone out here in the 'burbs had one—and searched for some Champagne, but there wasn't any. So yeah, I settled for whiskey instead. Mistake #1.

Mistake #2 was, after my third tumbler of liquor, logging back in and sending a message to LongDuck-Dong89 who was willing to offer me legal tender for inserting my finger up my rectum. It didn't seem like such a bad idea—I mean at the time.

It was easy, the dude sent a hundred bucks to my

PayPal account, my real one, I was too stupid then to have a second account. He sent the money before I even dropped my pants, but I was so drunk I did it anyway. Another video clip went up, this one of me jacking off with my right hand while my Crisco coated left index finger violated my virgin asshole. And you know what? It was pretty damn hot. I came hard, harder than ever before. Maybe that prostate stimulation bullshit wasn't such bullshit after all.

And the clicks poured in, the comments, and an email from some streaming porn site that wanted to pay me to mention them. "Sure, dudes," I slurred out loud, "send the dough and I'll shout you out." Who cared? The videos didn't show my face. I felt anonymous—free.

Mistake #3—no I didn't forget to wash my hands after fingering my asshole, mistake number three was that I popped a Xanax. And another. And washed it down with more Jack Daniels. I almost fell asleep, almost. But the neighbor's dog, that damn Chihuahua mutt they'd rescued or whatever was outside barking. It didn't stop, so I reached for my phone. "I'll call someone," I think I said, but I was hammered. And then the text came through:

Cal, come on, put on a tux and come on out. What do you have to lose?

What indeed—I'd pretty much lost everything.

So that takes us up to mistake #4—I put on my wrinkled Armani tuxedo and ordered an Uber downtown. Which took fifteen whole minutes—one of the disadvantages of living on the edge of the desert. As I waited, I watched my four new neighbor boys run around the street like a gang. Their mother, who I'd only seen in passing, was yelling about something, casing the block like a crazy person.

"Hey, have you seen our dog?" My door was cracked open, and somehow I let her make eye contact with me. Her long wavy brunette hair hung down her back, and I have to admit she had some decent curves to look at.

"What?" I asked, determined not to sound tipsy.

"The dog, she ran off again."

I realized there was no getting rid of this annoying woman, and my ride was minutes away anyway. She was a few feet from me as I locked my front door. One of her brood was running up, his face smeared with dirt.

"Uh, that fucking mutt?" I asked, glancing around the block.

"Language, there's a child here," she scolded, pointing to the boy. He was kind of cute, I admit, with his head full of curls.

"Sorry, that fucking *dog*?" I chuckled, and to my surprise she did too.

"I'm Barbara." She held out her right hand.

"Caleb," I answered.

"I'm sorry about all the barking and stuff. It's been... insane. My husband, um, he, left and we're staying here in my brother's rental house, and..."

I stopped listening to her as she continued her diarrhea of the mouth.

Eventually when I listened again she said, "The boys will be crushed if we can't find their dog."

"I'll keep a lookout for it. It was nice meeting you—I think that's my ride."

The shindig was a benefit for The Animal Foundation—but of course there were no actual homeless dogs and cats there. No, the A-List of Las Vegas wasn't going to risk having their designer clothes soiled. Instead, they paid a ridiculous amount for tickets, bid on auction items they didn't need, and in general walked around acting like they were New York socialites. Oh, and oops, Britney was there one more time. And no, she's not that innocent.

As soon as I had my first drink in hand, Jill was at my side. "Just like old times," I said as she looped her arm through me and walked me through the judgmental glares of my former peers. Everyone in that room, including my ex-wife, thought I'd had sex with a young client. They all thought the worst of me, and my silence about the whole thing hadn't helped.

"Michael is upstairs in the Amber Room—go up and talk to him, Cal. And please, tell him the truth."

"Uh, yeah, I will, in a minute. I want to just get my bearings first." The sneers from around the room were classic. Fucking rich people with nothing better to do.

We never made it up to the Amber Room.

Yeah, there were a lot more mistakes that night. I've lost count.

It took less than twenty minutes for me to have Jill in some side office on a desk, her skirt scrunched over her bony hips. I admit it was good—her sweet, sticky arousal coating my tongue just like old times. When I went in for my power move, I felt my stomach threaten to empty, but I ignored it and sucked her so hard I saw stars.

"Cal," she howled, "Cal! I'm gonna come!"

I chuckled into her softness, ignoring that dizzy feeling from the ten gallons of alcohol I'd consumed. "Not yet," I moaned, plunging my tongue even deeper into her.

She spread wider, her legs shaking in anticipation for the climax that was about to shatter her. Despite my short-comings, I was always good at "the stuff."

Just as she was about to release, her clit swollen, her pussy fluttering like a hummingbird, it happened. Yeah, you saw it coming. There he was—the Honorable husband-to-be watching the fucked up husband-who-was eating out his soon-to-be bride.

"Get out," he said to my back. There was no anger, no surprise, just the icy words of finality. "Get out."

I left there before Jill even closed her immaculately-waxed legs.

Thank God for the ease of Uber.

Within twenty-five minutes I was comfortably in my tidy master-planned community.

"Ah," my slurring said as I rolled over into my expensive memory foam pillow. *Memory foam pillow?* And then her wet tongue slid across my cheek.

"What the hell?" she asked.

"Uh." One of my eyelids strained to open, but the room was spinning and I clamped it shut again.

"What the fuck are you doing in my bed?"

"Um, what?"

I managed to pry an eye open and made out the pissed-off face of my new neighbor Barbara staring at me. And then she slid her tongue across my neck. No, not Barbara, but her little rodent-dog.

"Oh, God, um, I'm sorry, I must have showed up in the wrong..." And then it happened; a classic case of insult to injury. It started with a verp, then became a full-on hurl.

Yes, my new friends, I managed to end my clown show of an evening by emptying my drunken stomach into my neighbor's linens. And, oh yeah, the fucking dog attempted to lick it all up. Holy hell, why am I telling you this?

She should have kicked me out; hell, she should have called the cops, or even worse – posted it on Facebook. But no, Barbara brought a bowl and held my head while I emptied the sad contents of my stomach. As I drifted to sleep on her pillow, she swiped a cold washcloth across my forehead. We've been best friends ever since that night.

THREE
BUTTER ME UP

I DECIDED THE NEXT MORNING, as my body shook and my mouth felt like I'd swallowed a sweater, that I was done being a fuck-up. It was time to face life head-on and get my groove back.

That lasted about twenty minutes. Then I got distracted, and did some porn-surfing. Then I jacked off. And then, I got an email from *her*. The chick who got me in all this trouble in the first place. She needed more money. We'll get to who she is later. Much later. But just know that I barely had what she needed in my account, so...

Yeah, I sent it to her PayPal, but then I started thinking about the fact that I'd just jacked off for *free*. Maybe I could get more people to pay me for doing things on YouTube?

I took a shower and did some manscaping. There were comments on my last vid about "too much hair" and "time to whack the weeds" and shit. After I was all groomed, it was easy to jack off on camera. I mean really easy. Ridiculously easy, even sober this time. I posted it and watched the comments roll in.

And sure enough, harry_p_ness12 offered me a

hundred bucks if I'd show him my asshole—he didn't even ask me to violate it. I was high on my new power. Then I had an idea. What could I offer them for money?

"Does anyone want to buy my underwear?" I typed in my own comments. And sure enough, within five minutes JoBlow69 offered me two hundred dollars for them if he could privately watch me jump around in the undies for a few minutes. We exchanged emails, I made the private vid, and he sent me the money.

And by the third day in, I was a YouTube star. My comments and likes were off the charts, and more and more followers were offering me cash for various shenanigans. I even managed to pay off one of my credit cards. I never showed my face—I was completely anonymous. Life was good, what could go wrong? Yeah, right.

———

The next day, the course of my pitiful life changed forever.

"Sure you're shit-hot on YouTube, but it's limited, that's all I'm saying. Be smart about this, Mr. Drake."

This guy stood in front of me and never bothered to remove his sunglasses. He was short, at least a foot shorter than my six-foot-two frame, and skinny. Like tweaker skinny, like I could fold him in half skinny. Even worse, he wore a thirty-five thousand dollar vintage Rolex Daytona. Even when I was at the top of my game, I didn't have that kind of bank to spend on a fucking watch. I glanced down at my own beat up Omega and leaned back on the hood of my car—at least I still had a decent ride. My Porsche hadn't yet been found by the repo man.

"So what is it you're offering me, exactly?"

"Easy. You masturbate for my camera, and I'll pay you a

thousand dollars in cash immediately after that goo hits your belly."

"Who are you again?" This asswipe had contacted me through my YouTube channel and had been bugging me for a week to meet with him. I finally agreed to—outside of a Starbucks five miles away. No way I was going to be seen with this douchebag in Henderson.

"John Butters. I do the series *Butter Me Up*—it's part of my Gay for Pay brand."

"So wait, gay porn? Do I look homo to you?" I mean, I'm good with homosexuals—I know it sounds cliché, but my best friend is gay. No really, he is—and I'm good with that. But I'm not, well I mean, I wasn't then. Okay, back to the story. I told you I'm not very good at this storytelling thing.

"No," John Butters said that afternoon, lowering his Ray-Ban Aviator sunglasses to look me in the eye. "I'm seeking straight men to have sex on camera for money."

"Yeah, for gay guys to watch, right?"

He sighed and leaned against my car. Yeah, he parked his skinny-jeaned ass on the hood of my Porsche. "It's complicated. The majority of my viewership actually consists of heterosexual females."

"Wait a minute," I said as I tried to process this news. "So you want straight guys to go at it so women can get off on it?" I was incredulous—who knew?

"That is correct. I mean, sure we have some gay followers, but for the most part, our viewers are female."

"Okay, so you're offering me a wad of cash to jack off for women? I do that everyday for free."

"Exaaaaacttttllyyyy," he said, in his annoying, drawn-out way.

Of course I said no. In fact, I didn't even say no. I just left. That was the end of it. Well, I mean I thought it was that afternoon, anyway. I went home and made another YouTube video—my viewership was growing, and I was starting to see money from the clicks. Several big porn sites as well as The Love Store were running ads on my channel. But, the cash was still meager—nowhere near what I needed. And, even worse, that evening I got a warning from YouTube to take down my "pornography." Shit! And my last video was a giant hit—I decided to branch out from the normal cock pumping to a bit of butt plug ass play—don't judge me, they loved it. And to be honest, so did I. But now, they were threatening to pull the plug, pardon the pun, on my fledgling channel.

I glanced again at the last email from John Butters. "Just jack off for the camera," he'd said. "Just you."

But what worried me was the stipulation that I *had* to show my face. His series was about professionals, *straight* professionals, who performed for his nosy camera.

———

By morning the next day, I was fucked. I mean figuratively, not literally. Not yet anyway. When I went to log on, my account was gone. The plug was pulled—no not the buttplug, but the stream of income I'd gained was gone. I did the one thing I could do—I messaged John Butters and told him I was in. Or out I guess.

The instructions from Butters' assistant were to show up at the Orleans at two the next afternoon. They wanted me in a suit, and that was really it. Of course I showed up at two-thirty in ripped jeans and Chucks.

Butters looked me up and down, his hands stuffed in his ridiculously skinny jeans, rolled up at the ankle, before telling me to sit on the end of the bed. I remained standing. I've never been good with authority.

"So Caleb, I'm going to conduct a simple interview, easy questions. Don't give your surname for any reason." He stared at me as if I needed time to process.

"Got it," I finally said. I sat down on the edge of the bed. Not because he told me to, but because I wanted to.

"After the interview I'll pause the camera and put some heterosexual pornography on that monitor." He pointed to a screen over his left shoulder. "You'll undress, lie back on the bed, and masturbate for me. No semen, no dollars. It's that simple. I'll need you to sign this release, and also I need a picture of your driver's license."

I complied—he was wearing me down and I was ready for it all to be over.

And to tell you the truth, it was easy. So damn easy. He asked basic questions like "You're an attorney, right?" And my age, what brought me to Vegas (I was born here—some people *are* actually produced in the city). He wanted to know why I was willing to jerk off for money, and I simply answered, "Why not?" That was it—deep, intellectual interview. NOT.

I was pretty much semi-hard before I even took my undies off. I was ready to perform for his damn camera, and I'd decided to give him the best fucking jack-off he'd ever seen.

So I played it up—I teased myself, I played with my

balls, I even did my new trick of popping a digit up my rectum. I was a superstar at this. And it didn't hurt that my giant cock looked GREAT on camera.

When I finished I smeared my wad of cum all over my newly-shaven belly—I even thought about spiking the ball and tasting it, but I'd never done that before. Instead I looked over to Butters in a "How about that shit" victorious glance.

But he didn't seem that thrilled with my Oscar-winning performance.

"Thank you, Caleb, we all enjoyed your antics." His tone was dry, and he was already ending the shoot. "Cut," he said with a pissy eye-roll.

"What?" I whined as I cleaned my spunk off my skin with a towel he tossed me. "I was great!"

"You were adequate, and I will pay you. Thank you and have a nice day." He pulled out an envelope and counted out bills.

"Adequate? I was a porn star! What the fuck are you bent over?"

He handed me my wad of cash "Caleb, it was fine. I was just hoping for a little more...reserve, awkwardness. My series is about reluctant performances—I usually coax out the sex act. If you want to do it, at least right away, it loses some of that 'gay for pay' appeal."

"Oh," was all I could say.

I left disappointed. Maybe I sucked at the porn thing, pardon the pun.

———

But days later, he asked me back. Sure, Butters tried to sound breezy, but I could tell he wanted me. Besides, I'd already seen all the attention my jack-off scene got on his website—they loved it.

"So you want me back?" I asked when I called him back a respectable two hours later.

"Well," he said with that usual droll tone, "it would seem they liked your debut."

"They loved it!"

He sighed audibly into the phone. "It was the size of your member, Caleb, not your performance. I shall try you one more time, but this time only with another performer."

I bit the side of my cheek so hard I could taste the metallic tinge of blood. "I don't know..."

"Up to you. If you decide to let Chad suck you off, I'll pay you another grand."

"Wait, that's it? I mean you gave me that for jerking off —a dude sucks on my wang for the same price?"

"I always pay far more for a debut than the scene is worth."

"Two grand."

"One, and not a penny more. You decide—by tomorrow."

Click. *That bastard hung up on me!*

That night I sat in my driveway next to Barbara, as had become our custom since we'd become friends. She sipped on a tumbler of chardonnay as I worked my way through a six-pack of Stella. Her boys tore up the black asphalt on their scooters, the glow of their reflectors reminding me of my own childhood in Vegas. During the day, it's so hot the kids are cooped up inside, or worse, peeing in my pool, but at night it's always beautiful.

"So are you going to do it, Cal?" She leaned into my folding camp chair, her eyebrows in a knot.

"No."

"No, no or no, maybe?"

"No maybe," I confessed.

"I'd let anybody lick me for a grand I think." She took a long swig of her wine.

"I mean, yeah, it's just a fucking blowjob, right? Who cares? I'll close my eyes and think of a hot chick and the mortgage will nearly be covered for the month."

"So you're going to do it?" she asked with wide eyes.

"I honestly don't know. Can we talk about something else?"

She leaned back into her own rickety chair and stared at the sky. "So he called me last night."

"Douchebag?"

"My husband, Rob."

"Your cheating soon-to-be-ex-husband Douchebag, you mean."

"I know, I know. It's just—it's lonely out here. I have one friend—you, and you don't even like me."

I nudged into her shoulder. "I like you sometimes."

"Not enough. Maybe if I let him come over it would bring back memories, remind him of what he'll be missing. Hell, I'll even let him put it *there*."

"Lure him back with anal? You're twisted. You oughtta be doing that anyway."

"Oh, he tried the *accidental* peen-to-asshole tap a few times but I never let him put it in. But to get him back I'll do anything." Even in the faint glow of streetlights, I could see the pools of tears in her eyes.

"Listen, get yourself on Match-the-fuck-dot-com or whatever. Hell, get on Tinder. Get laid, but do not give yourself to that cheating asshole. And certainly don't give your asshole to that cheating asshole."

FOUR
MÁS TEQUILA

IT WAS four days before I was in a different hotel room sitting on the end of the bed next to some young guy I'd never met before. He seemed to not care one iota that he was about to suck my cock on camera.

"So Caleb, you're back again. What brings you back here?"

"Cash," I answered honestly. Well, maybe it was a bit more than that.

"And you, Chad? Why are you back?"

He cringed a little and glanced at my zipper. "Uh, my car payment is due."

"Excellent," Butters answered in his annoying-as-hell way. "Shall we start?"

That's the guy I told you about at the beginning of my sordid tale. Chad wasn't there to make a car payment. Well, I mean not *just* that. Chad was there because he loved to suck dick, and he loved to do it on camera. Like I told you before, he was so fucking *skilled* at it. He loved my dick down his throat—he wasn't rushing, he wasn't gagging—he was savoring it. That dude rolled his tongue up and down my ten-inch cock like it was a fucking lollipop. By the time he swallowed, taking the whole thing down his tight throat like no girl had ever done, I was about to shoot my wad. *Think about war, sick babies, puppies, think about anything...* But when Butters barked at him to play with my balls, I was done. It really was the best blowjob of my life up until then, and like I told you, I was hooked.

Even better, Butters was pleased as punch this time and asked me back the following day. It wasn't as good of a BJ as Chad gave, but one college sophomore from UNLV, the jock-type, devoured my dick as the other one licked my balls. I'll admit, this wasn't a bad way to make a buck.

———

I did three more scenes for Butters, all blowjobs, before he went back to Los Angeles. It was perfect, at least as far as gay for pay. I'd made a shit-ton of cash, and Butters said he'd call me when he came back to Vegas. Even though my hearing before the Bar was fast approaching, life was good.

When Butters returned to town, I made even more money. Otherwise I spent my days smoking by the pool with Barbara and the gang of neighborhood misfits we attracted—it was a glorious summer before it all went BANG that first week of August.

I'd just done a scene for Butters—he called it some weird sexual term, I forget what it was. Anyway, it was basically some guy sucking me off while another dude fucked him from behind. Fairly standard fare for Butters, and it was fairly entertaining.

I'd barely made it home and put my cash in the safe when she knocked on the door. Jill—standing there in her stilettos with a smug look draped across her artificially plumped up lips.

"What? I paid you," I snapped as she brushed past me and sat her new Louis Vuitton bag on my countertop.

"I saw him. Derek—he's in Vegas." The words were carefully planned as if she were giving a soliloquy in Freshman English class. Which, I might add, is where I first saw Derek Johnson.

I tried not to flinch; I struggled not to show that cold bitch my hand. But it was useless—I leaned back into the hard granite and stared at her.

"Derek, that's cool," I said, trying to sound as if I didn't care. But my heart was about to come out of my chest by way of my dry, hungover pie hole. The mere mention of my college roommate sent me into heart palpitations.

"Cool? Cal, *Derek is back*—he's living here in Vegas. And, I happen to have his number." Now her collagen-infused lips were really curled up into a smile, even though the Botox kept her middle-aged forehead as smooth as a baby's butt.

"Yeah, I'd love to, you know, go out for a beer with him, or whatever. Send me his 411."

"No one says 411 anymore, loser. I'll text you his details if you answer one question for me."

"What," I asked with a defeated sigh.

"Are you still in love with him?"

———

It took me two hours to recover. Of course, it took Jill about a zillion hours to recover from my refusal to stroke off for her viewing pleasure—the selfish bitch. Derek Johnson—my

college roommate, back in Vegas. It was too much to
process.

So by now I guess I have 'splaining to do. Yeah, I was,
well, um, attracted to another guy once, long ago. Okay
that's a lie—I was in love with my college roommate. All
those times Butters directed me to "think of her" I was
really "thinking of him." Just not any of the *hims* that were
offered naked and hard to me in that hotel room. Dark
skinned, latte-colored-eyed Derek Johnson, quarterback of
the less-than-stellar UNLV Running Rebels, was the one I
pined after scene after fucking scene.

And even worse, Jill knew it.

She'd caught us once, in college. We'd all been out
drinking, and we came back and collapsed into the same
bed. Me, my girlfriend, and the Greek-god Derek Johnson,
my roommate. Early in the morning, Jill woke up to pee and
said she saw my leg wrapped around his. I denied it all,
blamed alcohol and said I thought it was hers, but by then
Derek and I shared the same bed most nights. Here's the
thing though—we never had sex. We never even kissed—we
just, I guess we just cuddled for lack of a better term. We
shared an attraction, a symbiosis that got us through those
years. I got married, he went to law school out of state—we
just lost touch.

Okay, that's a lie. I dropped him like it's hot after gradu-
ation when Jill got pregnant. We married, she lost the baby,
but the distance between Derek and me was done. I tried to
cleanse the idea of being attracted to him, okay, of being *in
love* with him, away. But he was always there, like a specter
hovering in my subconscious. And now, he was back.

I did what we all do—I stalked him on social media that
afternoon. He was openly gay now—he had a boyfriend. A
freaking doctor—a gynecologist! What a waste... That was a

joke. His guy was beautiful and successful, and his Facebook was full of their wonderful life together. I wanted to shoot the ducking MacBook screen. I mean fucking, not ducking—that was autocorrect. Clearly I'll need to hire an editor for this manuscript or whatever it is.

But, back to that afternoon. I wanted to go through Derek's Instagram, but Barbara was at the door. I ignored her, so she went around to the back and peered through my French doors.

"Cal, open up," she howled, her fist pounding on my glass.

"I'm sick, I'm busy, I'm-I'm indisposed."

She wasn't buying it.

She kept banging my door until I opened it.

"You said you'd babysit tonight, remember?" She was nervous, shifting from one high-heeled shoe to the other like a bird on a wire.

"When the hell did I say *that?*" Seriously, she was on crack.

But it ended up being me who was on crack. Kid crack, that is. The runt of the litter, I mean her youngest, began to shit himself not more than twenty minutes after she left. I considered bringing the dog over to clean it up, but instead I just took him out back and hosed him down.

I'm kidding—I took care of it.

Luckily, for me anyway, she was back within two hours.

Once we got the kids to bed, I sat at her kitchen table as she pulled out the tequila. "I need a shot," she said. "I need lots of shots."

"What happened," I asked against my better judgment.

"He wanted to fuck me." She brought out the limes.

"Of course he did. That's what we want. What did you expect?"

"Dinner." She brought out the salt.

"Well, I mean, men are assholes, right?"

She nodded and did her first shot. I sat there shotless.

"It's been so long since I've been out there. I've been married to one man for fifteen years. And now, it's just," she did another shot. I still sat barren, dry. I got out of the chair and joined her at the kitchen island. I didn't want to drink when I had her kids, but now—that chick needed to lubricate me.

I did my first shot as she sucked down her third in three sloppy gulps.

"Cal, it's just, he's off with Bubbles or Bambi or some twenty-year old and I'm all old and shriveled and..." I held her as she sobbed, and when the tears stopped I put her to bed. Alone—I told you it wasn't that way between us and I'm a tiny iota of a gentleman sometimes.

FIVE

POTATO SALAD

"I'M REALLY NOT sure what this is about," he said as he slid his sunglasses off.

John Butters sat across from me at a local bar—Standard & Pour. I'd invited him there because I thought the open deck with a Vegas Valley view might impress him. Okay, that's a lie. I asked him there because they have a cheap happy hour and I was worried I'd have to pay.

"I'm just not clear on why you aren't using me this week. Did I fuck up or something?" I'd learned from the chatter on the *Gay for Pay* site that Butters was shooting in Vegas at the Rio, and yet I hadn't been asked to work.

His eyes narrowed at me. "Of course you did not fuck up. You are quite popular with my subscribers. However, this week I'm shooting all frat boys."

I nearly choked on my four-dollar Heineken.

"All perfectly legal—all performers over eighteen, signed releases and identification on record, blah blah blah."

"No, I get that. But I'm being shut out of shooting by pimple-faced, basketball-short wearing kids?"

"Exaccccttttlllly," he said, this time more smug than even usual. He was enjoying watching me squirm.

"Well, uh, next week then. I'll do more with that one guy—the smooth one."

He sipped his cheap bourbon before bothering to answer me. "Renaldo certainly does know how to wax. But what is this about, Caleb? Are you broke already?"

I wasn't, actually. For the first time in forever, I was financially on fairly stable ground, thanks to Butters.

"No, uh, I mean we can all use more money. It's just that..."

He leaned forward, that damn superior twinkle in his eye.

"You know, it's kind of fun."

I'd given him what he needed. Now he smiled and fell back into the plush chair he was perched in. He said nothing, but he couldn't stop with that fucking grin.

"Careful now, cowboy. If you like it too much, you won't be gay for pay anymore. You'll just be gay."

———

It didn't happen the way I'd planned. Nothing ever does.

I'd been stalking Derek's social media for a week, carefully calculating the exact right way to contact him. I composed countless messages, only to delete them. I finally decided I'd run into him Saturday night. He'd been tagged in a friend's Instagram photo as one of five going to a local pub for drinks—and his boyfriend did not seem to be among those tagged.

But of course my carefully planned accidental meeting didn't happen. What *did* happen was I ran into Derek Johnson during the day on Saturday—with potato salad.

Not *over* potato salad, but *with* potato salad. I creamed a ginormous plate of it all over his expensive-looking shirt.

It started the day before when Connie from the battered women's shelter sent me an email to remind me about the annual picnic. Food, those giant blow-up inflatables, maybe even a pony or some shit I assumed from her invite. And yeah, you're wondering what the actual fuck I would be doing at a battered women's shelter, but Sara's Sanctuary is what got me into this mess in the first place. Well, my career mess anyway.

I did legal work for them, pro bono. That's where I met Lillie—the girl I was accused of having an inappropriate relationship with. She's since disappeared, but even if she hadn't, I'd never ask her to take any sort of stand and tell the truth and bail my sorry ass out. I crossed a line—and I'd do it again any day, hands down.

So, back to the picnic. That shelter was the one social invitation I wanted to accept. They were good to me, and I did good work there. It felt way better than the personal injury shit I did for money. That afternoon, as I saw the email, I saw Barbara's kid in my yard with some freaking squirt gun shooting my damn cactus. *Willy, Wally, Walt— what the fuck was his name and why did she have so many damn boys?*

And yes, against my better judgment, I shot out a text to Barbara, my new bestie it seemed, and asked her if the boys might enjoy a picnic. Then she pissed me off by asking how much it would cost. *Jesus, this woman has been treated like shit,* I thought. *Free,* I answered. *You're driving, be ready at ten.*

So Saturday, long past ten, Barbara mounted up her crew, and me, into her battered SUV. At least she left that damn little rat of a dog in the house, wailing and destroying the blinds as we pulled out of our sun-baked neighborhood.

"How are your gay videos going," she asked as she merged onto the 15.

"What the fuck? Did you really ask me that in front of these kids?"

She shrugged. "They don't have a problem with homosexuality."

"Well, fine, but uh, porn might be an R rated convo, Babs."

She chuckled as her chestnut hair flopped over her shoulder. I loved her; I knew it that afternoon. No, no, no—not like you're thinking. More like kindred spirits—friends forever and all that bullshit.

So yeah, with the kids screaming at me like I was their dad or something, I smashed a plate of over-mustarded potato salad all over Derek Johnson. There was no limit to the fucking-up I could do.

As one of her brood pulled on the leg of my pants, he smiled. *That smile...*

"Cal! I was hoping to run into you. I've been doing some work over here at the shelter since you left. How've you been?" He was still smiling.

"Uh, yeah, I heard you were around again. Let's catch up."

He glanced down at whatever-his-name-is, sticky faced and dirty fingered, who was still tugging on me like I was behind on child support or something. "Uh, these aren't my kids, I just, uh, they are my neighbor's."

"I'm gonna throw-up," wailed the sticky, dirty spawn as we stared at him.

Yep, he hurled all over Derek's designer shoes.

SIX

PEE IN THE POOL

MIRACULOUSLY, days later I opened my front door to find Derek standing there.

"He cheated on me."

The words caught me off-guard, but not as off-guard as Derek's presence on my front porch. Even worse, I had Barbara and half the neighborhood out back. And, even worse than that, they were already drunk off their asses.

"More Coors Light!" shouted the guy from down the street, I forget his name—and as if I'd have Coors Light anyway.

"Just a sec," I shouted through the cavernous open floor-plan of my suburban mini-mansion.

I turned back to Derek, the faint hue of his eyes causing my stomach to lurch. "I'm sorry," I offered with a shrug. "Would you like a drink?"

"Cal, I think the dog took a tinkle in your pool. Should we shock it or something?" Barbara stood behind me, the shaking little dog under her arm.

"Shock the dog?" I was confused. "That seems extreme —I pee in that pool more than I do inside."

"Shock the pool, idiot. And now I'm thinking we should."

"Just take him home," I said without looking at her.

"I'm sorry." Her voice was shaky—I'm sure she was sorry, but I didn't give a rat's ass at that moment. My mind was still reeling over the fact that he was there, ready to talk to me.

"It's fine, Babs," I joked. She hated being called that. "Take the mutt home and bring back some Coors Light for Rick and we'll call it good."

She smiled. "Ron, his name is Ron. He's been your neighbor for three years."

"Ah, yeah." I never was good with names. The truth is I'm not good with names because I don't much care.

"Let's go out front," I said to the long-faced Derek after Barbara finally got the hint and went away.

He followed me toward the garage. "Beer?" I asked.

"Do you have whiskey?"

I nodded. This could get good.

Sitting in my driveway in two folding camp chairs, the noise of the pool party echoing in the dry air, Derek started talking to me. Over a bottle of Jack, he bared his soul.

"So his mother was sick. Great woman, I really like her. We were waiting for news on her bloodwork when his phone buzzed on the kitchen counter. I glanced down at it, and..."

"I'm guessing it wasn't mom?"

He shook his head. "Somebody named Giles thanking him for a great time."

"Giles? Who the fuck is really named 'Giles'? I mean in real life."

"Cal, he was on some dating app. I mean, they're called dating apps. For most gay dudes they are fucking apps."

"So you confronted him?"

"Yes, and he didn't even deny it. That fuckwad did not even give me the courtesy of contrition."

"Uh, that's fucked up."

He sighed and refilled his plastic cup from the bottle of Jack. "It's pretty normal actually in our circles. I just didn't expect it from him. We were about to adopt a child, for fuck's sake!"

"So he said what?"

"He said it was just sex and that he loves me. I asked him to stop, to promise never to do it again. He just laughed."

"He smashed your heart to hell? What a douche."

"No, he didn't." Derek turned and looked at me—those café latte eyes searching mine for some sort of reaction. "I don't love him, I never did. I realize that now—I loved the idea of him. Coming out was pure hell, but William was there for me. The idea of living with that sort of acceptance I guess, the illusion that we could be some sort of normal couple—that I loved. And losing it is what's crushed me."

We sat in silence until the sun set behind us, the noise of splashing and adults drinking, grilling, living rumbled around us.

"This seems like a great neighborhood," he finally said. "We've never met any of our neighbors."

"To be honest, I never really got to know any of them until this summer. Jill sort of sucked all of my attention."

"I hear that. That chick with the dog—are you two hitting it?"

"God no. We're just friends."

"Caleb Drake, friends with a woman," he said with a smile.

"Hey, I've changed. A little, at least. This whole thing has really altered my outlook on life."

"So what happened?" Derek leaned in closer, so close I could smell the spice of his cologne. The smell of him was more than enough to give me a raging boner.

I shifted in my seat, unable to avoid it any longer. I had to tell Derek.

"As you know, I was doing pro-bono stuff for the abuse shelter. This chick comes in one night, her face swollen, her lip cracked. Only here's the thing—she was underage, seventeen, and on top of that, it was her father that did that to her face."

"People are shit," he said, pouring more Jack into my cup.

"It gets worse, but I really don't want to go there now."

"How are you keeping yourself busy during the down time?" Derek looked at me, and I made the epic, I mean fucked up, decision to tell the truth.

"Gay porn."

"Not funny," he snapped, and before I could say *I'm an asshole*, he was gone. Gone. As I sat in my garage in a damn Eddie Bauer chair that Jill got free with her first SUV, I'd lost him again. I could smell the glory of his cologne as his tires squealed down around the cul-de-sac. *Slow down!* I heard the squall of mothers scream into the night at him. I'd lost him before I ever had him.

————

But the next day, my Facebook pinged with a friend request from Derek. I played it cool...for ten seconds before clicking on the accept button. Then there was nothing. No PM, no invitation to like pages, no anything. Just silence.

All afternoon I opened my messenger app, started to type, then closed it. I didn't know what to say, and every time I tried with Derek, I fucked it up. Instead of doing something smart, I took a shower, shaved as necessary, and drove to meet Butters for what he called "Attorney Caleb and Julian--Round 4." Yeah, he'd called me, but said he would only use me again if I'd perform anal sex on camera for the first time.

You'll judge me I'm sure, but I said yes. I needed the cash and the distraction.

SEVEN
CREAM PIE

"EXAAAAACCCTTLLLLY JULIAN," Butters cooed to the skinny kid who was pulling my belt off. "Beautiful enthusiasm." We were back at the shitty Orleans that afternoon for my first penetration scene.

Julian was eager—I could tell he loved sucking cock. The second my anaconda popped out of the top of my Calvin's, he was all over it. Licking, nibbling, *teasing*. This guy was good, and as much as I was enjoying his tongue polishing my knob, I was ready to fuck him.

And I actually liked it. Sure, I'd done that with women more times than I count, but with dudes, it was different. It was the main course, not some extra thing being done as a favor or even worse, in exchange for something. Jill once let me fuck her backside in exchange for a trip to see her parents. Yeah, for real—our relationship was fairly fucked up.

Julian, though, was so ready for my dick in his hole that I could taste it. He jumped up and dropped trou the second Butters directed him to strip.

"That's it, Caleb, stroke that giant cock," he instructed

as I lubed up. Butters paid extra for what he called "bare-back" and I'd finally gone through the testing, so I was allowed to fuck without a raincoat on.

Julian knelt on the end of the bed, his cock hard, his back arched. With both hands on his hips, I dragged him toward me. From the giant bottle on the nightstand, I squirted a ridiculous amount of lube on his ass. He'd need it.

When I slipped the head of my cock into his tight ring, he moaned. He didn't say "Oh fuck" or "Your cock is too big" or "Holy shit." He moaned. A slow, sensual, delicious moan that almost got me off before I'd even gone in an inch.

And he was still hard. I'd noticed in Butters' videos, most guys went soft when penetrated. But not Julian—Julian got harder the further I pressed into his tight, eager ass.

"More," he moaned, reaching back and spreading his round ass cheeks with both hands.

"You horny mother fucker," I said as I pushed as hard as I could, past the tight ring of resistance, as I call it, and deeper into him.

When I pulled all the way out and plunged back in again, I thought he was going to puke. He howled, he protested, but his dick never budged. After a deep breath, he said it again.

"More."

This kid was amazing. He couldn't have been more than twenty-three and during the interview we did before our scene, he said he was completely straight. Straight *and* married with a baby, even.

I was close to blowing my wad when he snaked one hand underneath him and started stroking off.

"Flip him over," Butters barked from the sidelines. Truth be told I'd forgotten he was even there.

When Julian rolled to his back, his cock still in his right hand, and scooted to the edge of the bed, I had to think of all my standard "do not come" scenarios. I stalled by applying more lube for as long as I could before Butters snapped his bony little fingers and pointed at Julian.

I glanced at the clock on the table. I was supposed to go ten more minutes—this scene was set as a "full scene" with no cuts and needed to be almost exactly twenty minutes. As tight as Julian was, I'd be lucky to make it twenty seconds.

His muscles tightened when I pounded into him again. With his hand pumping his own decent-sized member, he glanced at the clock. It seems I wasn't the only one trying not to come too fast.

"Kiss him," Butters said, his voice all lusty. I'm surprised that douchebag wasn't jacking himself off too. I'd never been asked to do that, and it shocked me more than the idea of sucking dick, the other thing I said I'd never do.

I ignored Butters and slowed my thrusts into Julian. His eyes were closed, his own hands moving slower. A fine sheen of sweat glistened on his forehead and across his marvelous chest.

"Whatever," I said out loud. Leaning in awkwardly, I tried to kiss him. The whole thing was a mess—I couldn't reach him, his eyes never opened, so instead I ended up just oddly hovering somewhere in front of his face.

I'm pretty sure I fucked up the scene, but Butters, I admit, was good at what he did.

"Julian, let Caleb jack you off."

I wanted to refuse to touch the guy's junk, but it seemed far less intimate than the kiss would have been. Besides, I needed the distraction—his ass was clenching me in that way that women do when you hit the G-spot.

Julian's eyes opened as my fingers touched his cock. "More," he said again in that moany, fuck-me-please way that was driving me insane. Yeah, I admit I was actually attracted to this guy.

I stroked him off, slowly at first, toying with the fluid leaking from his tip. The whole time my dick was firmly planted in his throbbing asshole, barely moving. When I sped up my stroke on his dick, his hips raised into the air. When I sped up, I saw him glance again at the clock. Two minutes—we were almost to the finish line.

"Faster," he moaned. "And fuck me harder."

And I did. I went at his dick like a piston, my own cock mercilessly pounding his ass, until he shot all over his own belly and chest—a beautiful sight. A sight so majestic, I missed my own shot.

I mean, I didn't miss my *shot*, I missed pulling out in time to show the world my junk spewing all over his junk. Butters didn't get the money shot I was supposed to provide.

But again, the guy is good. "Julian, that was so sexy. Let's have a closer look at the cream pie Caleb just gave you."

I just stared as the camera zoomed in to Julian's leaking asshole, pushing my frothy white spunk out of him and onto the bed. I was pretty sure I'd never eat a cream pie again.

After we'd cleaned up and gotten dressed, I followed Julian to the door. As soon as we were alone in the hallway, I did something insane. I mean I was possessed by demons or something. I asked him out. Or to hook up, or whatever they call it these days.

"Haha, dude, I'm like totally married and only into women. Thanks though, I'm flattered...I think."

Yeah, that was like a total rejection. "Oh yeah sure," I said without making eye contact. "It's just, uh, you know, we were pretty good in there."

He laughed. Not at me, but kind of with me. "Yeah, great scene. I try to give it all I have, Butters pays extra for that. I'm not working now—some legal stuff on my record—so I really need the cash. It's not hard to just *act* for me, but no, I don't bat for that team. Sorry, bro. I'm more than up for another scene sometime though."

He left, and I looked down and counted the stack of bills from Butters. Julian may have gotten extra, but I did not.

EIGHT
FLESH LOLLIPOP

"SO CAL, TELL ME ABOUT CLEANLINESS," Barbara
said out of the blue that evening. We were alone—the others
had gone to some concert. Her kids were, as usual, tearing
up the street with scooters as we sipped our drinks in my
driveway.

"I have no idea what you are talking about, as usual."

"Cleanliness. When you do the gay porn stuff."

"Shhh! Could you keep your fucking voice down? You
think I want grumpy grandpa across the street hearing
that shit?"

"Sorry. I just mean...with anal—is there never any..."

"Mess?"

"Yeah, like, how do you know there won't be dark
matter."

"Oh, that. I haven't done that part, but I saw somewhere
that they have this long protocol—enemas and stuff to make
sure there are no surprises. I think they are on liquid diets
even or some crazy shit up until the scene."

"Hm, I'll have to remember all that. I plan to offer up
my backside to Rob this weekend."

I shook my head. "Offer up your fine ass to someone more worthy than that lying, cheating dickwad, Babs."

"Don't be so dire. I was hoping you'd offer up some tips on de-flowering the forbidden zone so I'll be prepared."

I took a deep breath. I really liked Barbara, but I often wanted to shake her like a ragdoll. She had no idea what she had to offer some lucky guy someday.

"You know, go slow, lots of lube, but to be honest, I've never received, only pitched—so I have no idea about that part of it."

"Would you ever?"

"Fuck no." But in the back of my mind, I knew there was one person I'd let do *anything* to me, anytime. And he was back in town.

———

It didn't take long for me to bug Butters for another scene. Yeah, I for sure wanted to do more fucking on camera. But that's not what Butters offered.

Instead, he said he'd give me two thousand dollars to suck a dick. Now it was getting real. I'd told Butters from the beginning that I never pitched; I would only receive. But I needed that two grand before the mortgage was due.

"It's easy," Barbara said that night in my backyard.

"Easy? For you maybe. I bet eating pussy wouldn't be so effortless."

"It's more difficult sure, but I've done it for free. Two grand? I'd lick half of Vegas."

"What if I gag?"

"They'll like it even more if you gag."

She was right. I took a long swig of my bottle of beer

and watched the kids splash around the pool. The pool that Jill made me build for the kids we'd never have.

When Jill lived here, it sat unused. But now, after Barbara's boys had become frequent guests, on any given night I'd end up with all of the neighborhood kids in there. Annoying as fuck, but it was sort of comforting to not be alone.

"Fine then, I'll try it I guess."

"Pretend it's a lollipop," she advised before screaming at one boy to stop shoving the other's head into the pool skimmer.

The next day, I found myself doing yet another interview for Butters. His voice droned on, grating on my nerves. I just wanted to get it over with and get my cash.

"So Caleb, you've never sucked anyone off before, correct?"

"Fuck no," I snapped, nervously glancing over at Charlie, my gay for pay partner for the next hour or so.

"Have you ever wanted to?"

"No," I lied. *Don't think about Derek.*

"Well, let's start by undressing," Butters directed as he always did.

I was relieved that "Charlie Cox" had an average sized dick, but getting him hard was a struggle and I wasn't putting my mouth on a flaccid dick. The thought of it made me want to puke. If it were hard, I could close my eyes and imagine the lollipop thing like Barbara suggested.

Eventually, Charlie managed to get it up to a passable

semi as a particularly rough heterosexual porn movie played in the background.

"Caleb, kneel in front of him, let's get this going." Even Butters was impatient with the not-gay-enough-for-pay Charlie.

When my tongue hit his cock, I did think of a lollipop. But, I confess, as my eyes closed, as it slid into my mouth, I couldn't help but pretend it was Derek.

I'd seen Derek's erect cock once. I mean, we were college roommates, so I'd seen a lot but that one time, that one glance, was seared into my memory.

I'd left class early and when I opened the door to our shared dorm room, the bathroom door was open. He was in the shower, his sweaty football gear sprawled all over the floor.

I took a chance, and before I could stop myself I glanced in. The shower door was steamy—but I could see it. A giant puff of soap bubbles shrouded it, but it was erect. Erect and big. He didn't jack off or anything, but as he toyed with it through the soap bubbles it got even bigger.

The thought of his large hands on that perfect cock made me salivate, and as I remembered that afternoon, I worked harder at sucking off the hesitant Charlie. I ignored Butters constant requests for me to open my eyes, but I did suck that mediocre dick off like a champ.

Mercifully Butters didn't make me swallow that day. In a small act of kindness, he ended the scene with Charlie jerking off on his own hairy belly.

As I left the hotel room minutes later, a wad of cash in my hand, I thought again about that afternoon back in college. Derek looked at me—he'd seen me watching him and he'd smiled. We never talked about it, and it never happened again, but I knew he'd like me to do to him what I just did to some random guy in a cheap hotel room in front of a thousand subscribers.

———

After sucking off Charlie, I stupidly called Jill and begged her to meet me for lunch. Why? Barbara was gone all day doing frivolous shit and I had few friends I could talk to. Okay, by "frivolous shit" I mean taking her kids to the dentist. I can be a bit narcissistic. Big surprise there, right?

"Cal, you have to stop. What if there's an ethics violation?" Jill stared at me with her lasiked eyes, her botoxed forehead as emotionless as her soul.

Yeah, when I called she came, I mean not sexually, I mean said she met me for lunch and I'd stupidly told her about the videos. Oh, and about that whole licking the snatch thing her ancient hubby-to-be saw that night at the gala? It took her all of a week to come barking up my tree again after that fiasco. I was dead to him, but somehow Jill survived the great cunnilingus at the gala incident unscathed. Judge Wapner probably knew she was a filthy whore and didn't care.

I sat across from her at Panera Bread pushing my plastic fork around some protein bowl.

"Next time let's go someplace for lunch that serves drinks."

"I'm trying to detox—it's clean food." She stabbed her own plastic fork into a cherry tomato and popped it into her mouth.

"Clean food for a dirty slut," I said.

"Oh come on, you called me because you want me." She

tried to grin seductively, but the green kale shit on her bleached-white teeth only repulsed me.

"I called you because...well, everyone else was busy. Besides, I thought maybe you'd still help me with the Bar hearing. That thing at the gala was your fault."

"My fault, sure. Caleb, perhaps you shouldn't have arrived drunk off your ass. The whole Hunter S. Thompson act is getting old."

She was right.

"Listen, I'm only going to do the porn thing a few more times to get back on my feet."

"Uh huh," she chuckled. "I think you like it. Speaking of liking it, I saw Derek again the other day."

I nearly dropped my chunk of clean food. "Where?" I asked before I could stop myself.

She batted her fake eyelashes. "At the courthouse. Why don't you just call him? Ask him out."

"I'm not gay."

"Of course not. Call him, Cal."

————

That night, after I'd shat out all the "clean" food, things changed. My maid, the one named after a president, I forget which one, came by. Not unusual, but this time she had a guy with her.

"So, um, Kennedy said you might have some good weed?"

Kennedy! That was her name. "Nope, fresh out," I lied.

She stared at me with that look—that *you're full of shit* look.

"Nah, it's fine," the guy said with a grin. Dirty blond hair swished across his forehead, and as his pale blue eyes met mine, I admit I got a little hard. Suddenly he appealed to me more than Reagan did—I mean Kennedy. I have to write that down.

"I might be able to dig some up. C'mon, follow me upstairs."

Kennedy squeezed the guy's hand at the mention of *upstairs*. We'd done threesomes twice before—I knew that's what she was up to when she showed up at the door with this guy. And I'll admit, she's pretty fucking great in the middle. This guy, Ryan he said his name was, though, he was different than the other nameless dudes. Ryan I wanted to see naked.

It started like the time before. The three of us sat on my master bedroom balcony and smoked weed while the sun set. And hey, I fucking hate when someone tells a story then has to go all into some damn detail of a sunset and shit, but if you've never seen the sun set in the desert sky over the mountains, you haven't lived. So bear with me this one small indulgence, or skip the next paragraph and move on to the sex stuff.

My house is on the edge of a cliff and looks out over the open desert. From my upstairs balcony especially, you can see the entire Valley. The barren desert to the left, the Spring Mountains directly in front with the interstate cutting through in the distance as all the tourists drive back to LA, and to the right the soon-to-be twinkling lights of the city of Las Vegas. We covet a Strip view here, and I had a killer one. Neighbors slowly stumbled out of their viewless houses to the end of the street to share a small portion of the view I had. If you don't have a phone full of pics of sunsets, you don't live here. Anyway, this sunset was stunning—the fire in the sky kind we get when it's a little bit cloudy and there's a haze from fires in California. I'm not a writer, so I can never describe the colors, but do yourself a favor and at least once view a sunset over the open Mojave Desert with your own eyes.

Okay, back to the sex. After the sunset, we opened another bottle of wine and smoked another joint. We were pretty loose—Ryan's bare feet were inches from mine. Something about his feet...God, he was pretty.

Kennedy eventually stood up and took my hand, pulling me toward my bedroom. "Cal is a great fuck, want to watch us?" she said to Ryan. He nodded.

It didn't take long for us to be naked. Before my greedy tongue made it to Kennedy's wet snatch, Ryan was tugging at the button-fly of his ripped jeans. I licked her like hers was the last pussy on earth—I licked her as if I actually liked her. And it was beautiful, but I couldn't help but look back at Ryan—bare-ass naked and kneeling on the edge of my bed.

He was lean, just like the guy I'd fucked a few days prior on camera. But unlike that guy, Ryan was perfect and there because he wanted to be. For Kennedy, of course, I reminded myself. But we all knew there was more. I looked once more at the dusting of golden hair across his chest and turned back to the eager snatch I was supposed to be eating out.

I made her scream. I made her pull my hair. I made her shake like the San Andreas. I made her squirt all over my face. That girl could come like a freight train, I'll always give her that.

And, when she was finally done, I slid in to fuck her from behind as she rolled over to suck Ryan's delicious dick. I was a bit jealous, and I really hated sucking dick. His eyes met mine, and I hate to admit it, but we both pretty much lost sight of her entirely.

And then it happened. He leaned down, I leaned up, and I kissed him. A guy, a dude. A person of the male species that I was neither being paid to interact with and who was not Derek.

Did I want to date Ryan? Spend my life with him? Even *be* with him like I wanted to be with Derek? No. But at that moment, in my bedroom, high as a kite, I wanted to have some sort of *intimate* thing with another man and not for pay. I mean it's easy now to analyze it all, but at the time I was kind of busy.

I pulled my soaked cock out of Kennedy and watched as they both sucked me off, together. I came all over both of their tongues, even sharing it with them in a big communal kiss. I couldn't deny it anymore—and it sure as hell wasn't about Kennedy and Ryan. It was about me.

I decided to call Derek. But, of course, first we gave Kennedy the best DP of her life, and yeah, I fucked Ryan twice that night—once with Kennedy's dirty little tongue straight up my asshole. Hey, you didn't expect me to get romantic before I had a little fun, did you?

So the next morning, after the Dirty Duo left, I called Derek. Yes, I called him. I didn't even text him to warn him first that I was going to call, as is, of course, standard protocol now days. And brace yourselves for the happy ending to my fucked up story of a life—except sorry, this isn't it.

The call went to voicemail, and I hung up. After making the world's strongest coffee, I decided to drunk dial him later on instead. Then, of course, that stupid voice of reason in my head talked me out of that. I picked up my phone again and sent him a text.

Hey, I just wanted to say that...all these years... I just can't stop thinking about you and wondering what might have been. But maybe now this is our chance? Call me or something. Plz.

And then I freaked out and tried to delete it, but it was too late. I about shit myself waiting for that "read" status to appear. It took twenty excruciating minutes for Derek to read my text. And it took twenty hours for him to answer it.

NINE

A MCGRIDDLE AND DEREK

NOTHING from him that whole day. Nothing from him that whole night. I stayed dead sober so that I wouldn't sound sloppy when he called. But he never called.

The next day I had a shoot with Butters. Some big group orgy scene—yeah, I'd advanced to that. I was bareback qualified and all by then. I was pretty damn gutted that Derek didn't want me, and I was determined to fuck him out of my memory that afternoon, and make a lot of money doing it.

I'm also going to break some writing rule my new literary agent told me about—don't go from one sex scene straight into another. But pretty much, this is how it happened, so this is how I'm going to tell it. Writing rules be damned—I can't write anyway and no one will ever read this freaking memoir, story, or whatever it is.

Oh, and also on the way to Caesars, I ate a giant Egg McMuffin. Okay, I ate that and that freaky thing where the syrup is in the bread—with extra bacon. I didn't care—my pooper wasn't the one being violated that day so I could eat. You see, those who get anal go through an extensive cleaning process before these shoots and then they are on a pretty much liquid diet until the shoot is over. Mess isn't sexy on-screen, and Butters wouldn't tolerate anything but a squeaky clean rectum. But I'm digressing now, because I sort of don't want to tell you what happened next.

So stuffed full of McD's, I sauntered into Caesars Palace. That's a lie. I was worried. Worried and pissed off, and yeah, hurt beyond belief, that Derek hadn't answered. Nothing. Not even a "fuck off, Cal." But normally, without the Derek thing, I would have sauntered. I was so full of my damn self at that point that I was actually comfortable making Gay for Pay videos. My bills were caught up, Jill was off my back—life was good. I mean other than Derek. And, of course, other than the fact that I was probably about to be disbarred, or at a minimum sanctioned, for an ethics violation I didn't commit. And yeah—we were shooting at Caesars that day versus the half-shitty Orleans where we normally shot. Butters had a doctor coming in for the scene and he wanted this one snazzy.

So that was a long paragraph for me, but I'm still stalling. I really don't want to write this. Oh, and no, Derek wasn't in the scene if that's what your dirty little drama-seeking minds were thinking.

The shoot was fine. Doctor Barton was hot—smoking hot, if that's still a saying. Butters was thrilled that I was willing to kiss finally, and the two of us made out in our clothes with hard dicks grinding. The doc was into me—he wasn't gay for pay, he was just gay.

And I loved it—except every time I closed my eyes you know what I saw. Who I saw. Derek—he'd haunted me for half my life and now my need for him was at a crescendo. And he still hadn't called. So I was determined to fuck him away with this hot doc and the two other dudes who were waiting terrified in the corner. Those two rednecks needed drug money—they really were gay for pay. I kind of felt sorry for them, but let's not get too serious because well, I really don't want to think about that part of it.

Back to the scene. I made out with the doc until Butters told us to get undressed. We awkwardly broke the kiss and tugged at our clothes. Unlike scripted porn, there really weren't any smooth transitions in Butters' stuff. He edited them a little, took his voice out sometimes, but the whole "we're just in a room banging for money" vibe was always intact. Anyway, the doc and I got naked and we were both already hard.

The two barely-legals in the corner looked a little calmer when Butters gestured for them to enter the scene. Despite the fact that they reeked of cigarette smoke and bad decisions, they were decent looking guys. I'm pretty sure they were loaded up on X or whatever else allows a straight guy to consider being fucked by some dude for a video.

The tweakers got naked, and the doc and I made out one more time—our chests pressed against one another, dicks hard and grinding. I really wanted to fuck him, not the tweaker I was supposed to pound. But even that was ruined —Derek floated through my mind again, but this time it didn't stir me up. It made me go limp when I thought about the rejection from him. He was never going to call.

The doc helped me out—stroked me back to a plausible semi as the new guys hovered around us without a clue what to do. Butters was slipping—I think he was as distracted by the doc as I was trying to be.

We managed to coax the newbies into sucking us off for the camera for a decent amount of time before we flipped them face down on the mattress. Side by side we lubed ourselves up, we lubed them up, we lubed to the ridiculous because these bros had no idea what they were about to get. Unlike normal intimate anal, there wasn't a lot of prep in these scenes. I didn't even buy the guy dinner before popping the head of my cock into his vise-grip like asshole. *Sorry dude,* I thought as he groaned.

The doc's guy was doing a little better. I mean, he had less to handle for sure, but he also seemed a little more in the zone. His dick was even hard—he stroked it as the doc shoved further and further into the guy.

My guy, however, was locked up tight and his tiny dick was as flaccid as a dead fish. "Kiss him, Caleb," Butters offered, his mind finally back in the game. But that wasn't happening—I wasn't about to kiss this kid. I was still only about an inch in—the anaconda-like squeeze threatening to ruin my hard-on. I threw him a bone, I mean, yeah, bad pun. I reached around and held his limp pecker in my hands.

"Close your eyes, think of your girl," I whispered to him, hoping Butters would edit that part out.

He clenched his eyes shut as I reached around and stroked him. Slow and easy, soft enough to stir his reluctant penis out of hiding. He moaned as I pushed in further, past the clenched resistance and far enough for Butters to purr, "That's it."

I had him fully hard by the time Butters barked, "Fuck him."

And I did. Not hard, not deep, but I did. But I didn't enjoy it—this time was different. As I flipped him over on his back, his eyes were still clenched together. What happened next was the end for me. His eyes opened, and I could see the shame in them. With that one look, I knew that what I was doing wasn't always without consequences.

I decided right then I was done. I'd had some fun, but maybe not everyone did. I assure you I'm the last person who is going to wax serious here, but yeah, that afternoon in that hotel room I decided my porn career was over. I mean I still love porn and all, I just never wanted to feel again like I did that afternoon.

After I'd cleaned up, I glanced at my phone. He'd answered me.

Cal, I want you. I need you. I might even love you.

But no, it didn't say THAT. Of course not. It simply said:

Call me.

Call me. I fucking hate it when someone texts me to call them. What is the point of that? But this wasn't just someone. This was Derek Johnson. This was the man I couldn't stop thinking about day and night. This was *him*, and I was so freaked out about it that everyone was staring at me.

"Uh, I gotta go, guys," I managed to mumble as I fled the room.

I didn't think; I just walked. As soon as I was away from the pack, I pulled out my phone. But I didn't need to dial—Derek was standing at the end of the hallway. And he wasn't happy.

"Oh, uh, hi, um...how did you..?"

"Cut the shit, Cal. I've seen you."

"Um, what? Seen me what?" I was about to puke. *Why was he here?*

"My cheating boyfriend showed me a video yesterday. Low budget online thing—guess who was starring in it?"

All of the bones in my body turned to soup and I evaporated into the garish wallpaper. I wanted to die, and yet I was alive. Alive, still greasy from the lube that never washed off easily, and standing in front of the one person I really wanted to be with. And he knew.

"Cal? Why?" His dark eyes were locked somewhere on the side of my face. I couldn't look at him.

"Why do you think? Money. How did you know I was here?" Somehow I'd managed to regain control of my body, but I still wanted to die.

"Easy. I looked up the guy's shooting schedule. There's a thing on his website. There aren't better ways to make a buck? I mean, shit, *Chippendales* is hiring or something." He was still staring at the side of my burning face.

"Uh, I mean, I don't really have the abs for *Chippendales. Thunder* maybe." He didn't laugh. He didn't move. I still couldn't look at him.

"To each his own," Derek finally said. His eyes left my face, and he turned to go.

To his broad, strong back, I said, "Don't go, let's talk."

He kept walking as I bleated out a sad, "Please." He kept walking. He never turned around. I was too lame to follow him. I let him go.

TEN

LET'S WRAP IT UP

TWO DAYS after Derek walked away, I was still in bed. Barbara came over, busting in as she usually does. Okay, that's not true; I left the door unlocked. Anyway, she came over and tried to drag me into the shower, but I just curled up like a burrito into my dirty comforter and moaned.

Three days after Derek, before the coyotes came to drag my corpse away, there was a knock at my front door. A knock, not a ring of the doorbell as is suburban custom. A fist was striking my door—loudly.

"Barbara, get the fucking door," I yelled to the air. She'd gone to Albertsons to get me something, I forget what, probably my self-respect. It didn't matter—I didn't need anything. Except him.

The knocking continued. BANG BANG BANG. Then the voice. "Caleb Andrew Drake, open this fucking door or I'm busting through the window."

Derek.

Oh my God, Derek was at my door. He was here. And I smelled like Fremont Street on Sunday morning. *Oh fuck! But he's here!*

Shower, fast, I thought. But it was too late—he didn't need the window. The front door was open. I rarely locked it up here in the hills—I mean, after all, crime is illegal in this posh master-planned community.

Derek was in my house. Derek was walking up my stairs. Oh shit, Derek was standing in front of my smelly, un-showered carcass. Derek was looking at me with those eyes. And he wasn't alone.

She stood next to him. The girl who got me into all this shit in the first place.

"Cal, I'm so sorry." Her pale eyes were rimmed in red—she'd been crying.

I wrapped my arms around her. "Lillie, it's not your fault."

She sobbed as my eyes met Derek's. "We didn't..." was all I could manage to say.

"I know." He sat down at the end of the bed. "She told me everything and is prepared to go before the Bar on your behalf."

"She can't do that. He'll find her, kill her."

"I called that judge—Jill's guy, he's willing to help."

"He'd help *me?*"

Derek nodded. "We are going to do a video testimony, get her to sign an affidavit, then she can go back into hiding. She'll be gone before anyone even sees it. She'll explain why she was at your house that night, why you gave her money, why you continue to."

"Tonight, now," I said. "Then she goes back."

———

So that's how it went down. Judge Wapner, I mean, the very

forgiving Honorable Michael Allen with my savior, my soul-
mate, my everything, Derek, saved my bacon.

That night, as she gave her recorded testimony in
another room, I sat on an over-priced Italian leather sofa in
the judge's chamber. "Gay porn?" Derek finally said.

I nodded. "Yeah, you know, it seemed like a good idea at
the time."

He laughed—the best sound I'd ever heard. His hand
drifted to my knee.

"I was shocked, that's all. I didn't think you...I just
couldn't wrap my mind around it all." We sat there like that,
his hand on my knee, for several long moments.

"How did you know? About Lillie?" I asked into the
silence.

"She called me while I was working at the shelter. Lillie
heard about the trouble you were in and wanted to help. I
never doubted you, Cal. Just for the record."

"I need you, Derek." The words were out loud, not in
my head like I intended them to be.

"That's a lot to process. Let's start here."

And yeah, it happened. He leaned over and kissed me.
It wasn't sexual, it wasn't foreplay, it wasn't even full of
tongue. It was his perfect lips, soft and full, gently stroking
across mine in a kiss that would forever change both of our
lives. And no, there's no big sex scene I plan to relay about
us. It's kind of private, and didn't really even advance to
that until a month later anyway. That night, though, was the
beginning.

Oh, and I guess I need to tell you what happened that
started all of it anyway, so here goes. It started with Lillie
Maynard, the broken, battered teen who sat across from me
in the intake room of the shelter. I helped her legally get

away from the monster who was destroying her, but through the beauty of social services and the juvenile court system, they sent her back. That was sarcasm, just in case it was lost.

On the night she was supposed to go back, she disappeared. I mean, she disappeared from the system. Lillie showed at my house—broken and terrified. She was never going back to the demon who gave birth to her. She told me her boyfriend was willing to drive her to Utah to hide with an aunt, but she needed cash.

I provided it. And continue to provide it, and will until she's old enough to not need me. That's another reason why I was so broke. I don't regret it, not for a second. See, you thought I had no redeeming qualities. When they questioned me about it all, of course I denied any knowledge of her whereabouts. I continued to deny it even as they combed through my financial records and found the payments. They threatened contempt, and I still stayed silent.

It got worse after she disappeared. A shelter worker, one who didn't like me much, jumped on it to accuse me of having an inappropriate relationship with a minor—that's all it took to start the Bar investigation.

Anyway, in the end, I wasn't disbarred, but I did receive a formal sanction and a fine—a fine which I did not engage in a porn performance to pay for. As far as Derek, that night was only the beginning, and we've certainly had a lot of twists and turns along the way. Suddenly switching teams wasn't easy for me, but somehow we've made it through and we're still in love today as I sit at my battered MacBook and type out my pathetic story. I gave up my career chasing ambulances and work full-time for the shelter for very little pay, but I love it. Oh, and well, my story isn't completely pathetic—I found the love of a lifetime.

———

THE END

———

ALSO BY SAM JD HUNT:

Santino the Eternal

Taken by Two

Torn from Two

Deeper: Capture of the Virgin Bride

Deep: A Captive Tale

Dagger: American Fighter Pilot

The Hunt for Eros

Roulette: Love Is A Losing Game

Blackjack: Wicked Game

Poker: Foolish Games

KEEP IN TOUCH

Amazon: www.amazon.com/author/samhunt
Facebook: http://www.facebook.com/SJDHunt
Twitter: @sjd_hunt
Instagram: www.instagram.com/sjd_hunt/
Goodreads: https://www.goodreads.com/SJD_Hunt

www.sjdhunt.com

A SAMPLE OF TAKEN BY TWO

An already-in-progress excerpt from the Amazon Top Three Bestselling Erotic novel *Taken by Two*:

"Penny, what the fuck?" Strong arms were lifting me, carrying me—but my heavy eyelids wouldn't open, my parched lips were sealed shut. I'd been ridiculously unprepared for my attempt at escape, and ended up wandering the harsh jungle for hours and hours until I somehow tripped and fell. I don't remember where I landed, just being very thirsty and confused.

I'm not sure how far he carried me. In my dream-like state, I wasn't sure if I was alive or dead. My head pounded, my heart fluttered. Nate's angelic face floated by my thoughts, his steel blue eyes comforting as he called to me. Rex's deep voice vibrated from somewhere near, whether real or imagined, I'm still not sure. "Hang in there, baby girl, I've got you," he reassured me that afternoon.

It all went dark for a long time, and then a blinding light flooded my vision. My head was in a thick cloud, pounding and pained. The light burned, and yet his fingers were forcing my eyes open. "Penelope, say something."

I struggled to open my eyes. Rex was hovering over me, the unmistakable look of concern in his eyes betraying his normal coldness. "I–I got lost, I was thirsty, fell into the river...so chilly..." I shivered, despite the brutal humid heat of the jungle around us. A scratchy wool blanket was wrapped around me. It was dark—I managed to tilt my head —we were in a tent. A tiny tent; my escape plan had been an epic failure. *What would he do to me now?*

"You're dehydrated, suffering from exposure. Falling into the river probably saved your life, sweetheart." Rex's normally harsh voice was soft, deep and swaddling as he spoke, his fingers brushing across my forehead. "Good thing I gave you a typhoid shot."

"Shot?" I was beginning to awaken.

"The other day, in your room. The injection was a typhoid fever vaccine."

A cold cloth wiped over me, followed by cool water at my lips. "Drink a little more, sweetheart." I fell back into a sound, dream-filled sleep.

"I'll be okay?" I was awake again, after what seemed like hours of comatose sleep, and sitting up on a sleeping bag in the tiny tent. Rex sat across from me on the ground, his fingers raking through his hair. He nodded, his dark blue eyes rising to mine, a faint smile betraying his feigned anger.

"Tell me you didn't harm Nate." His words were icy cold, severe—he couldn't mask his concern for his —for Nate.

"I took the key from his jeans after we..."

"Why the fuck would you leave the compound? We're

trying to keep you safe. You managed to escape from the good guys, Einstein, and almost got yourself killed in the process."

"I-I...I was kidnapped! You had me locked in a room against my will, then forcibly gave me a shot of something— oh yeah, and before that you stuck me in a canvas sack. And, of course, you *murdered* a friend of mine."

"What? *Murdered?*"

"The bartender you disposed of? I've known him for years." I couldn't believe I was arguing with a cold-blooded killer.

"I paid the guy off to not mention your leaving Vegas to have a tryst with some guy—I convinced him it would ruin the dude's trust fund and piss off his family. I didn't *hurt* your bartender."

"So you're not a killer?" I sniffed, struggling to under- stand it all with my dehydrated, fuzzy brain.

He relaxed, his hand wiping across my cheek. "Well, I wouldn't go that far. I didn't harm the bartender, anyway." He shook his head, and said with a grin, "You're such a pain in my ass." He gave me another sip of water, and said, "Ah, Penny, you have no idea the amount of trouble you've caused me today." He smiled at me despite his scolding words. "One more sip of water, then we'll try a little bit of Gatorade." He held the bottle to my lips tenderly.

"How many days have I been in this tent?" I wiped my lips as I looked around.

"All afternoon."

I was confused; surely I'd been floating in and out of consciousness for days. "That's all?" He chuckled again and nodded.

My head was pounding, my throat felt like I'd swal- lowed cotton. "I need a doctor," I begged.

He sat down on the sleeping bag next to me and pulled me into his arms. "I *am* a doctor, sweetheart."

When I awoke again, it was darker yet. The silver glow of moonlight illuminated the tent as I glanced around. Rex was next to me, my head on his chest. I sat up and debated whether I should run, but quickly abandoned the idea of escape. If Rex wanted to harm me, he wouldn't have spent all day nursing me back to health. He scared me, but I was beginning to understand him. He was far more bark than bite.

His eyelids popped open when he sensed my move-ment. I'd reached over to drink from a plastic bottle—the flat, sweet liquid tasting like heaven. "Little sips," he warned as he sat up. I nodded, setting the bottle back down. "I feel so much better. Can I go back?" He shook his head and looked at me with pity. "Penny, it's not safe for you to go back to Vegas. Right now, I can't even get you out of Colombia."

Colombia—we were in Colombia. That's not an island!

"Okay..." I believed him. "But can I go back to the house? It's not that far, right?"

"You wandered for miles, and I have a group of five men out there expecting to be led into the deep jungle to learn survival skills. They pay me a lot of money to teach them this shit. Looks like I have a new student." He poked me in the ribs. "I've already had to make up a story about who you are and why you are here—plus we've lost almost a whole day's trek while you recovered. I'll do my best to go easy on you, sweetheart, but welcome to hell."

After several more sips of Gatorade, Rex convinced me to sleep a few more hours until sunrise. As we lay back down together on the small sleeping bag, he offered, "If it gets too hard out there for you I'll call Nate to come get you when I get a signal. Try your best, though, Penny. I don't want Nate out here if I can avoid it—this group isn't the best crowd for him to be around—he's still vulnerable. The rest of the staff can't be trusted with you out here alone." *Vulnerable? To what?*

"Vulnerable," I repeated with a yawn. Suddenly, it all clicked. The physical intimacy between these two very alpha males, the level of trust Nate had in Rex, the protectiveness shown by Rex of Nate. *Nate must have some illness!* "*Oh*, you're his *doctor*," I said out loud.

Rex rolled over to face me in the pre-dawn blackness. "I swear, Princess, most of the time I have no idea what the actual fuck you're talking about. *Whose* doctor?"

"Nate's—I thought you might be lovers, but now I get it."

"*Lovers*—that's quite a ridiculous word. No, sweetheart, I'm not his *doctor*. Our relationship is far from a professional one, and none of your goddamn business. If you must know, I was once a field combat medic, but my *practice* quickly morphed into something much more...*classified*. Now go the fuck to sleep, or I *will* feed you to the snakes." The now-familiar threat of being tossed to reptiles, which had terrified me for days, I now realized was simply his twisted sense of humor. I refused to admit to him that my phobia of slithering creatures, especially snakes, was certifiable.

I wanted to ask more about Rex's past, and his relationship with Nate, but either he was fast asleep, or pretending to be in order to ignore me. Still processing the last few hours with this enigmatic man, I nudged up next to him, inhaling the manly scent I was beginning to like—like *a lot*.

"Morning, sunshine!" He was shaking me and yanking at the sleeping bag. "Get your lazy ass up, we're moving out." One of my eyes opened. Rex was hovering over me, agitated and threatening. "Now!" he hissed. His semi-sweet bedside manner from the night before had dissipated with the rising of the burning sun. "Yes, sir," I grumbled, sliding from the comfort of the covers.

He reached into a pocket and pulled out a tiny bar of something. "Breakfast," he said as he opened the crinkly wrapper. I reached out for it—I wasn't into granola bars, but I was starving. "We're sharing it, sweetheart. This is all the food we have until we catch lunch." He broke off a third of the bar and tossed it toward me. "You don't share so fairly," I mumbled as I chewed at the bland, dry cereal bar. "You're a third my size, you get a third—fair is fair. We could wrestle for it if you'd rather?" He winked at me as he devoured his share in two bites.

"Follow my lead out there—if word gets out that Penelope Sedgewick is here, we're all in trouble." I nodded, rolling up the sleeping bag. "Where can I pee?" I asked sheepishly. My head still throbbed, but at least I finally had enough to drink that I needed to release it.

"I'll take you, but can you wait two secs while I pack up?"

In minutes, the tent and all of his belongings were packed into a heavy backpack. I was tossed a flimsy day-sack before he led me toward the group of campers. The anxious men hovered around us in a circle—staring. None of them spoke until Rex gestured to one of the younger ones. "Joe, can you start the guys walking—head due north. We'll catch up." He turned to me and pointed toward some tall vegetation near camp, "That way, *sis*."

"Sis?" I asked when the others were out of earshot. "I

told them you were my step-sister, Joanie. After I found you yesterday, I quickly made up a story that my mom was staying with me and kicked you out into the jungle. I couldn't think of any other reason I'd have an unprepared woman out here." After walking several feet into the dense foliage, he pointed to a flattened area. "Sorry, no running water for you, Princess."

I was used to luxury, and had never camped out before, but I'd been known to party hard and squatting to pee outside wasn't new to me. Rex stood in front of me with his hands on his hips waiting. "I can't go with you watching!" I complained. He sighed in exasperation before turning his back to me. "You're high maintenance, lady. I've seen your lovely waxed snatch twice already, who the fuck cares if I see you piss?" I managed to lower the too-tight borrowed jeans enough down my thighs to squat and pee, Rex fidgeting the whole time impatiently.

"I need to wipe, do you have...?"

He sighed again before exhaling, "Grab a leaf, and do try to avoid one with something that bites on it."

I reached for a nearby frond of some lush palm—it did work fairly well as impromptu toilet paper.

"I'm not high maintenance. It's not easy to just let loose with someone watching." I zipped the jeans and stood. Rex turned to face me, and in one quick motion pulled open the button-fly of his canvas cargo pants. "It's a bodily function, sweetheart, it's nothing special," he barked. My eyes were glued to his crotch as he flopped out the most massive penis I'd ever seen in my life—in person, anyway. Even flaccid and wrapped in his gargantuan paw, it was still larger than life. With no regard for my gaping stare, he produced a loud, heavy stream of urine onto the verdant jungle floor. "See?" I couldn't answer—I was speechless at not only the size of his dick, but at the metal running across it—I wasn't exactly innocent, but I'd never seen a pierced penis in person. He gave his gigantic member a quick shake and shoved it back into the canvas pants. I didn't see any sign of undergarments—just King Rex and his enormous pierced cock—commando. "You're lucky we have plenty of drinkable water—if we didn't, that would have been your morning coffee, Princess," he added, pointing to the pool of urine near his feet.

Available in paperback, Amazon, and Kindle Unlimited.

Buy Taken by Two, US
Buy Taken by Two, non US

And don't miss the conclusion, *Torn from Two*.

Buy Torn from Two, US
Buy Torn from Two, non US

9 781977 744210